This book belongs to

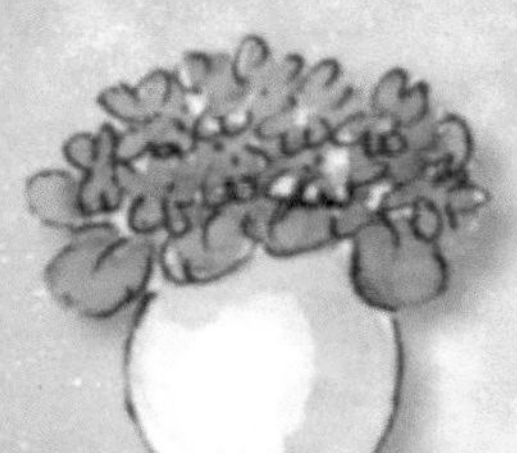

____

For Princesita Violetita, the smile in my heart.

May you explore the wonders of the world and mirror the perfection of you.

Thank you:

Frossene and Larry King, for your amazing friendship and invaluable help.
Michael, my son, for your input and for being the original smile in my heart.
Romi Caron, děkuji and merci encore, you are an extraordinary artist.

Publisher's Cataloging-In-Publication Data (Prepared by The Donohue Group, Inc.)
Names: Kahn, Denise, author, designer. | Caron, Romi, illustrator.
Title: Violet's voyages. Book 2, Greece : the dolphin adventure / story and design by Denise Kahn ; character illustrations by Romi Caron.
Other Titles: Greece : the dolphin adventure
Description: [Albuquerque, New Mexico] : 4Agapi, [2021] | Title from cover. | Interest age level: 002-012. | Summary: "Violet always starts her adventures by catching a ride on a shooting star! To what area of the world will it bring her? She hangs on tight until destination, where she is welcomed by a special local animal who is on a mission. In Greece : the Dolphin Adventure (Book 2), Violet meets Delphinaki and helps him with the quest"--Provided by publisher.
Identifiers: ISBN 9780997823172 (hardback) | ISBN 9780997823189 (paperback) | ISBN 9780997823196 (ebook)
Subjects: LCSH: Dolphins--Greece--Juvenile fiction. | Underwater exploration--Aegean Sea--Juvenile fiction. | Meteors--Juvenile fiction. | CYAC: Dolphins--Greece--Fiction. | Underwater exploration--Aegean Sea--Fiction. | Meteors--Fiction. | LCGFT: Action and adventure fiction.
Classification: LCC PZ7.1.K187 Vig 2021 (print) | LCC PZ7.1.K187 (ebook) | DDC [E]--dc23

ISBN 9780997823172 (hardback) | ISBN 9780997823189 (paperback) | ISBN 9780997823196 (ebook)

Visit: DeniseKahnBooks.com

Violet's Voyages

Greece: The Dolphin Adventure

Story and Design by Denise Kahn

Character Illustrations by Romi Caron

GREECE

Violet closed her eyes and quickly fell asleep.
In her dreams the stars winked at her.

Oh, how she wanted to touch them!

Violet saw a shooting star and reached for the sky. She caught it and held on tightly.

Violet loved going on adventures and rode the star until she arrived in Greece. She marveled at the ancient sites like Delphi, also known as Pytho and the center of the world.

And the monasteries of Meteora, so high they seemed to touch the sky.

Violet continued her journey and saw Athens
with the Acropolis guarding the city below.

Violet loved the beautiful islands with their white-washed houses, surrounded by the famous Greek blues of the sky and sea.

Violet stood on a sandy beach and looked into the crystal-clear water.

Suddenly a dolphin squealed and bopped his head up and down at her.

She waved at him and said:
"My name is Violet, what's yours?"

"I'm Delphinaki," the young dolphin said. "I can't stay long, I'm on a mission. Would you like to come with me?"

"Oh, yes," Violet said, wading into the water. "Where are we going?"

"To look for the ancient temple of Delphin. Climb up!"

Violet scrambled up his back.

As they headed toward their mission they passed several islands.

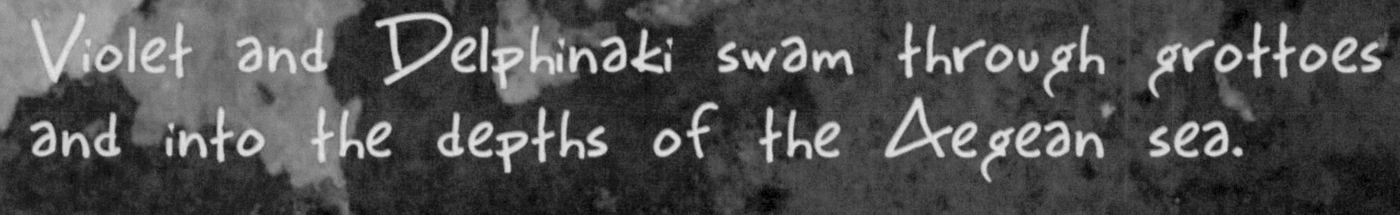
Violet and Delphinaki swam through grottoes
and into the depths of the Aegean sea.

Violet held on tight and marveled at the sea creatures as they swam by.

"There it is!" Delphinaki exclaimed.

"It's very beautiful," Violet said.

"It's probably around 4000 years old."

"That's really old."

"There are dolphin statues!" Violet exclaimed.

"That's because this is the temple of Delphin, God of the Dolphins."

"Look at the pot!" Violet exclaimed. "Oh, and I like the runners."

"That's an amphora," Delphinaki said. "They were used to carry liquids, like oil or water and have pretty drawings on them."

"Yes, from the ancient Olympic Games, which started over 2000 years ago here in Greece. Oh, and on that one there's my owl buddy Sophos, which means wise."

"And dolphins!" Violet added gleefully.

"Here's one of a Goddess and she looks like you," Delphinaki chuckled.

Violet held on to Delphinaki as they headed back to the little island.

Violet and Delphinaki lay on the sand next to each other. They were tired from their adventure and started falling asleep as the water gently splashed over them.

"I bid you Irini. It means Peace in Greek," Delphinaki said.

"And we are also known for our Filotimo, which is love of honor. But it means much more. It is also honesty, good behavior and morality. It is a word that only exists in Greek", Delphinaki continued.

"Well, Irini and Filotimo to you too, my friend," Violet said.

Violet woke up the next morning and saw an amphora from the temple of the dolphins! Hadn't it been a dream?

Violet wondered where the next shooting star would take her, and who she would meet.

THE END ...until the next voyage!

Follow Violet
on her adventures
around the world!

About the Author

Denise Kahn created Violet's Voyages series for her granddaughter. She hopes Violet and other children will enjoy these stories in lands around the world as much as she loved creating them. Denise believes there is no stronger bond than sharing a book. Her desire is for her work to entertain and inform and that her readers, from 3 to 103 years young, cherish reading and discovering together.

In addition to her children's series Denise also writes for adults in several different genres: Romance, adventure, metaphysical, military and historical fiction. Her books have been bestsellers and featured on television. Early family experiences have provided the basis for Denise's story themes and settings. She lived in Europe for over twenty years while her father was a diplomat with the U.S. State Department. Her mother was an opera singer and Denise's very first memory of life was her Mom's glorious voice singing to her. She attributes the music, which plays an integral part of her novels, as the 'glue' that holds the stories together.

Denise is a linguist and speaks several languages fluently. She is also an audiobook narrator with more than fifty titles, her own as well as other authors'.

Her proudest accomplishment is being the mother of a gallant Marine Veteran. Among the household Louie, the cat, believes he was a king in a previous life.

For more information check out Denise's books and audiobooks:

DeniseKahnBooks.com / DeniseKahnVoices.com

Books by Denise Kahn

Children's Series

Violet's Voyages - Switzerland: The St. Bernard Adventure (Book 1)
Violet's Voyages - Greece: The Dolphin Adventure (Book 2)

KKO Keeping Kids Occupied: Over 500 Ideas and Activities

Travel Tales

(Short travel stories for all ages)
We were 12 at 12:12 on 12/12/12 (Mexico)
Entertained by the Gods (Greece)
Sai Baba's Ashram Rendezvous (India)
Gstaad Grace (Switzerland)
Thanksgiving in 24 Hours (Mexico)
Olympic Honor (Italy)

Novels

Peace of Music
Obsession of the Heart
Warrior Music
The Music trilogy
Guitar Woman (Novella)
Split-Second Lifetime
Hot Air
Enchanted Football

Photo Book

Around the World in 80 Quotes on Photos

DeniseKahnBooks.com / DeniseKahnVoices.com

Made in the USA
Columbia, SC
18 March 2025